FROGGY GOES TO CAMP

FROGGY
GOES TO CAMP

by JONATHAN LONDON
illustrated by FRANK REMKIEWICZ

SCHOLASTIC INC.
New York Toronto London Auckland Sydney
Mexico City New Delhi Hong Kong Buenos Aires

For Aaron, Sean, Claire, Eli, Jordan, Natalia, Annie, Abby, Yasha, Michael, Bill,
Jonathan, Arielle, Elaine, Laura, and Maureen
 —J.L.

For Jack, keep on singin'
 —F.R.

ISBN-13: 978-0-545-16570-9
ISBN-10: 0-545-16570-9

Text copyright © 2008 by Jonathan London. Illustrations copyright © 2008 by Frank Remkiewicz. All rights reserved. Published by Scholastic Inc., 557 Broadway, New York, NY 10012, by arrangement with Viking, a division of Penguin Young Readers Group, a member of Penguin Group (USA) Inc. SCHOLASTIC and associated logos are trademarks and/or registered trademarks of Scholastic Inc.

12 11 10 9 8 7 6 5 4 3 2 1   9 10 11 12 13 14/0

Printed in the U.S.A.   40

First Scholastic printing, May 2009

Set in Kabel

It was summer.
Froggy woke up
and jumped on his bed—*boing!*
boing! boing!

He was so excited,
he bumped his head on the
ceiling—*bonk!*—
and fell down.

FRROOGGYY!

called his father.
"Wha-a-a-a-t?"
"Up-and-at-'em!
Today's the day you go
to Camp Run-A-Muck!"

Froggy hopped out of bed,
got dressed—*zap! zip!*
zoop! zup!
zut! zut! zut!—

and flopped into the kitchen—
flop flop flop.

"Have you got everything?"
asked his mother.
"Of course!" said Froggy.

"Let's go!" said Dad.

And off they went.

"Oh, no!" cried Froggy, an hour later.
"I forgot my sleeping bag!"

"Oh, Froggy!" groaned Dad,
and turned the car around.

Two hours later, "Oh, no!" cried Froggy.
"I forgot my bathing suit!"

"Oh, Froggy!" groaned Dad,
and turned the car around.

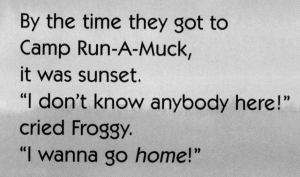

By the time they got to
Camp Run-A-Muck,
it was sunset.
"I don't know anybody here!"
cried Froggy.
"I wanna go *home*!"

"Come meet your bunkmates, dear," Mom said.

"Welcome to Camp Run-A-Muck!"
said Jordan, his counselor,
and led them to Froggy's cabin.
It was named "Wildcats,"
but his bunkmates were the
two Toad twins
and an otter named Yasha.
Yasha was nice—he let Froggy
have the top bunk.

"Look!" said Mom.
"There's your principal, Mr. Mugwort!
He's the camp director!"
"Great," said Froggy. "Not!"
By the time his parents waved good-bye,
the moon was rising over Lake Winnemucca.

At sunrise, a bugle blasted—
da-da ta-DOT ta-daaa!
"Last one up," said Yasha,
"gets tickled with a feather duster!"

Froggy was the last one up—
"Hee-hee! Ha-ha! Ho-ho!"

"Welcome, campers!"
announced Mr. Mugwort.
"Now, listen up!
Today's your swim test.
Tomorrow, swimmers will
race to the raft on the lake—
at the crack of dawn!"

But now it was time for breakfast.
Froggy had K.P. duty—Kitchen Patrol:
washing dishes, preparing veggies and flies,
and serving.
When he served Mr. Mugwort,
two fried eggs slid off . . .
right on Mr. Mugwort's head—*splat!*
"Oops!" said Froggy.

Froggy passed the swim test—
of course.
Later, he had archery.

He pulled the bow . . . aimed . . .
let go—*twanggg!*—
and hit Mr. Mugwort's bottom—*thwap!*
"Oops!" said Froggy.

On Tuesday, the bugle blasted—*da-da ta-DOT ta-daaaa!*—
and Froggy flopped down to the lake—
flop flop flop—ready to race.

FRROOGGYY!

called Mr. Mugwort.
"Wha-a-a-a-t?"
"You forgot your bathing suit!"
Froggy looked down.
"Oops!"

He was wearing his boxers.
Everybody laughed—
even Mr. Mugwort.

On Wednesday, they went on a big hike
around Lake Winnemucca.
It got so hot that Froggy said,
"Let's jump in the lake with all our clothes on."
Jordan, the counselor, did a swan dive . . .
Yasha did a jackknife . . .
and Froggy did a cannonball . . . *splash*—
and got Mr. Mugwort all wet.

On Thursday, in the dining hall, the Toad twins yelled,
"Food fight! Food fight!"
and everybody joined in.
Froggy threw a banana, but Yasha ducked . . .
and it smeared across Mr. Mugwort's shirt—*smoosh!*
Mr. Mugwort was not a happy camper.

On Friday, Mr. Mugwort asked,
"Who knows how to paddle a kayak?"
(He was also the kayak instructor.)
"I do! I do!" cried Froggy.
"Are you *sure*?"
"Yep!" Froggy put on a life jacket
and sat in the front.
Mr. Mugwort pushed off
and climbed in.

Uh-oh! Froggy held the kayak paddle like a canoe paddle and dug in. *"Y-i-i-i-i-i-i-i-i-i-kes!"* And over they went—*splash!* "Oops!" spluttered Froggy, looking more red in the face than green.

Mr. Mugwort glared at him . . .
then laughed and hollered,
"Water fight! Water fight!"
He handed out squirt guns . . .
and they had the wildest water fight
in Camp Run-A-Muck history—*splish!*
splosh! splooooosh!

And that last night, they stargazed . . .
told scary stories around a bonfire . . .
and sang camp songs, like,
   "Dear Mama Duck
   Dear Papa Duck
   It's fun here at
   Camp Run-A-Muck. . . ."

When Froggy's family came in the morning,
Mom said, "How was camp, Froggy?"
"Great! I hit Mr. Mugwort with an arrow!
Smooshed him with a banana!
And capsized our kayak!"
"Hmmmmm, that's nice, dear."

And Froggy sang,
"*Dear Mama Duck,*
Dear Papa Duck,
It's fun here at
Camp Run-a-Muck!"
a-a-a-a-a-l-l the way home.